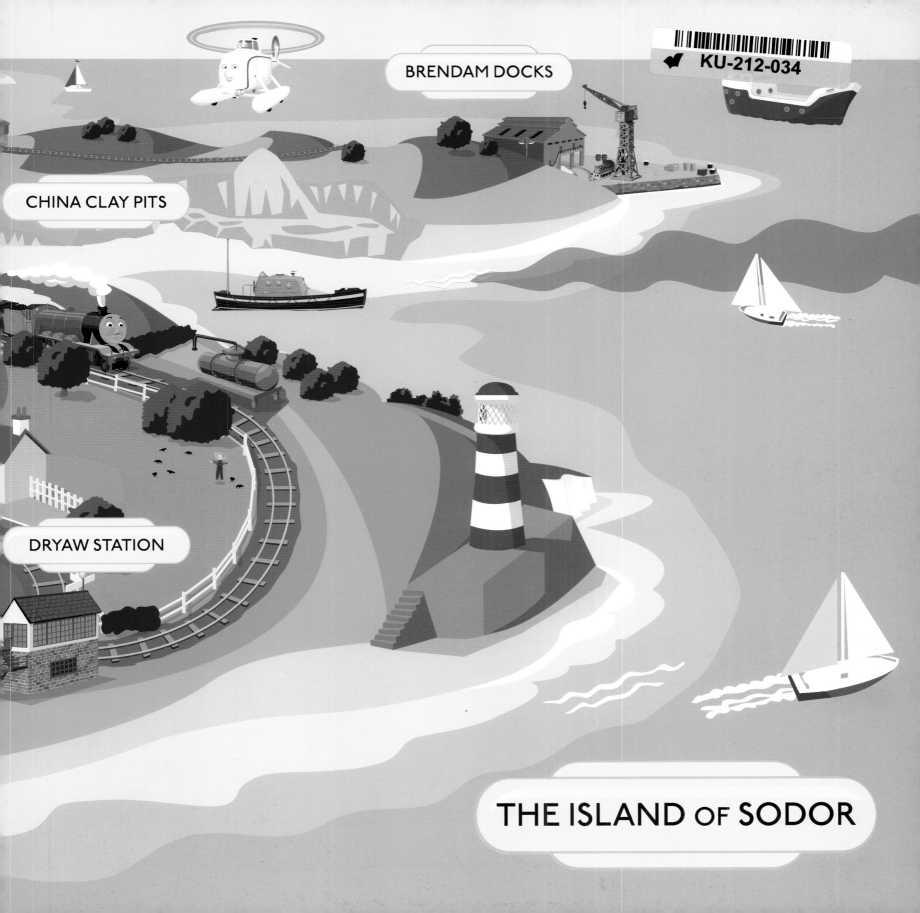

BRENDAM DOCKS

CHINA CLAY PITS

DRYAW STATION

THE ISLAND OF SODOR

First published in Great Britain 2022 by Farshore
An imprint of HarperCollins*Publishers*
1 London Bridge Street
London SE1 9GF
www.farshore.co.uk

HarperCollins*Publishers*
1st Floor, Watermarque Building, Ringsend Road
Dublin 4, Ireland

Written by Laura Jackson
Illustrated by Robin Davies
Map illustration by Dan Crisp

CREATED BY BRITT ALLCROFT

Based on the Railway Series by the Reverend W Awdry
© 2022 Gullane (Thomas) Limited.
Thomas the Tank Engine & Friends ™ and Thomas & Friends ™
are trademarks of Gullane (Thomas) Limited.
© 2022 HIT Entertainment Limited. HIT and the HIT logo are
trademarks of HIT Entertainment Limited.

ISBN 978 0 7555 0412 1
Printed in Great Britain by Bell and Bain Ltd, Glasgow
001

A CIP catalogue record for this title is available from the British Library.

MIX
Paper from
responsible sources
FSC™ C007454

Thomas and the Muddy Mishap!

This is the story of when Thomas needed help from a very special digger ...

It was the day of the Invention Fair on the Island of Sodor.
Sir Topham Hatt had given the engines important jobs to do.

Alfie wanted to help, too.

"These jobs are best left to the Steam Team," said Sir Topham Hatt. **"You're a digger, Alfie. Digging** is what you do best."

Alfie loved being a digger, but he sometimes felt his job wasn't important. He wanted to be like the Steam Team.

"Thomas!" Alfie called out. "Can I help you with your job?"

"I'm carrying heavy loads today," Thomas **puffed.**

"You're built for digging, not pulling flatbeds!"

So Alfie went to ask Nia if he could help her with her job.

"Sorry Alfie, I am collecting cargo today," said Nia.
"You can't travel on the tracks."

Suddenly, Gordon **whooshed** on past. "Lots to do, lots to do!" puffed Gordon.

"Can I help with your job?" Alfie called after him.

"I am picking up passengers," said Gordon. "And you're not built to carry passengers."

Poor Alfie. Nobody wanted his help.

He **chugged** slowly back to the construction site.

"Maybe diggers can't do important jobs after all," Alfie told Jack.

"Digging is important, too," said Jack, kindly.

But Alfie didn't feel important at all.

Meanwhile, the Steam Team were busy with their jobs.

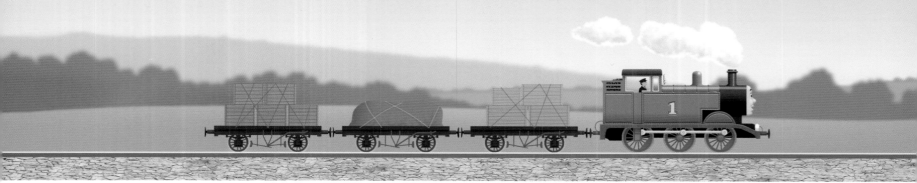

Clickety-clack, clickety-clack! Nia pulled the cargo.

Faster, faster, faster! Gordon collected his passengers.

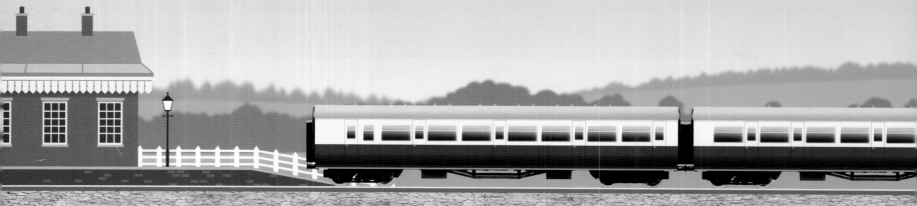

Peep! Peep! Thomas **raced** up and down to the fair.

Thomas was on his last delivery of the day. He was taking the prize trophy to the fair.

"Woah!" Thomas called out as he raced around a bend. He was going too fast.

The trophy **slid** off the flatbed and Thomas came off the tracks.

He landed with a **squelch** in a muddy bog.

"Help!"

Nia and Gordon soon heard Thomas' cries for help. But Thomas was **stuck so deep in the mud,** the engines couldn't reach him.

This job was **too big** for even the Steam Team.

Then Thomas had an idea. He suddenly knew exactly who could help.

"Nia, we need a digger!"

Over at the construction site, Alfie was busy digging
when Nia **screeched** around the corner.

"Alfie!" she puffed.
"We need your help.
It might just be the most
important job on Sodor today."

Brrmmm! Alfie raced up to the crash site as fast as his wheels would go.

"Muddy rescue here I come!" he sang out.

In no time at all, Alfie was doing what he did best. Digging!

Dig-a-dig-a-dig!

Soon Alfie had freed Thomas from the mud.

Rocky the crane arrived
and **lifted** Thomas back
onto the track.

"**Thank you,** Rocky and Alfie,"
Thomas blushed, but then he
looked worried. "**The trophy!**
It's still in the mud."

Another dig was no problem
for Alfie. He dug until he
saw a **glimmer** of
gold in his scoop.

"**One muddy job
complete!**"
beamed Alfie.

A very **muddy** Thomas and Alfie finally **rolled** up to the Invention Fair. All the passengers cheered when they saw Alfie with the trophy in his scoop.

"You rescued Thomas, and you saved the fair, Alfie," said Sir Topham Hatt. "Everyone has an important part to play on Sodor, including diggers."

Alfie suddenly felt **proud** to be a digger.

He might not be able to ride on the tracks or pick up
passengers, but Alfie could dig. And being a digger
was a **big** and **important** job after all.

"**Hooray** for Alfie!"
Thomas cheered.

Peep!
Peep!

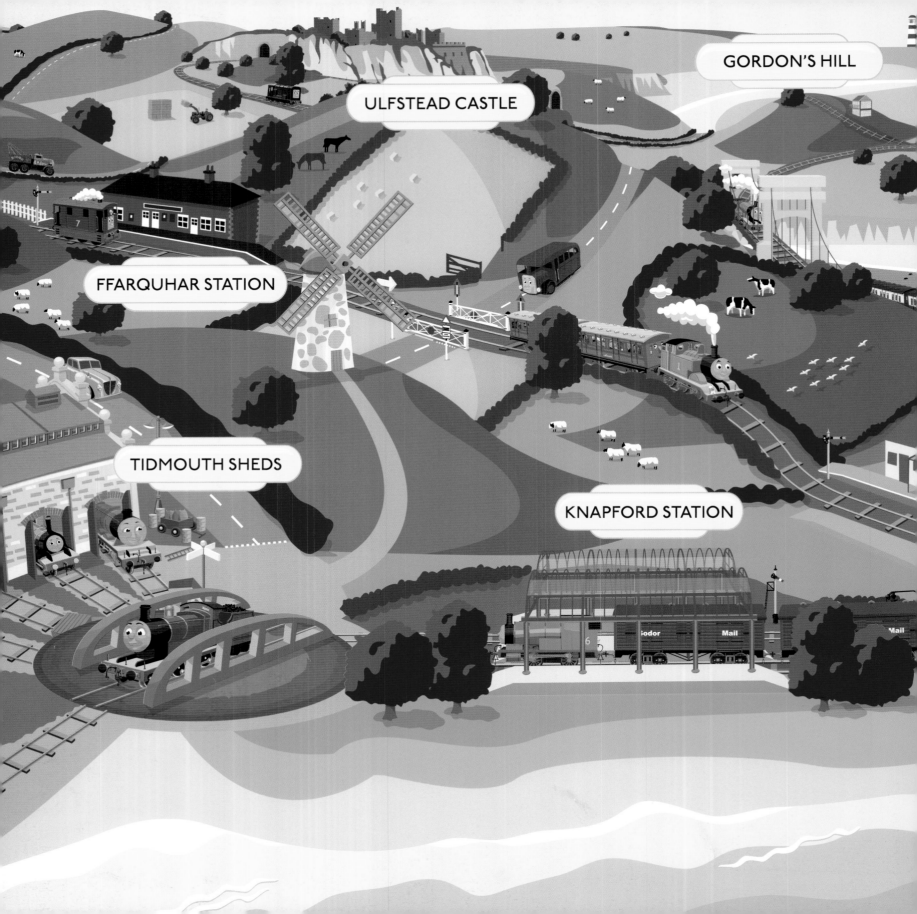

GORDON'S HILL

ULFSTEAD CASTLE

FFARQUHAR STATION

TIDMOUTH SHEDS

KNAPFORD STATION

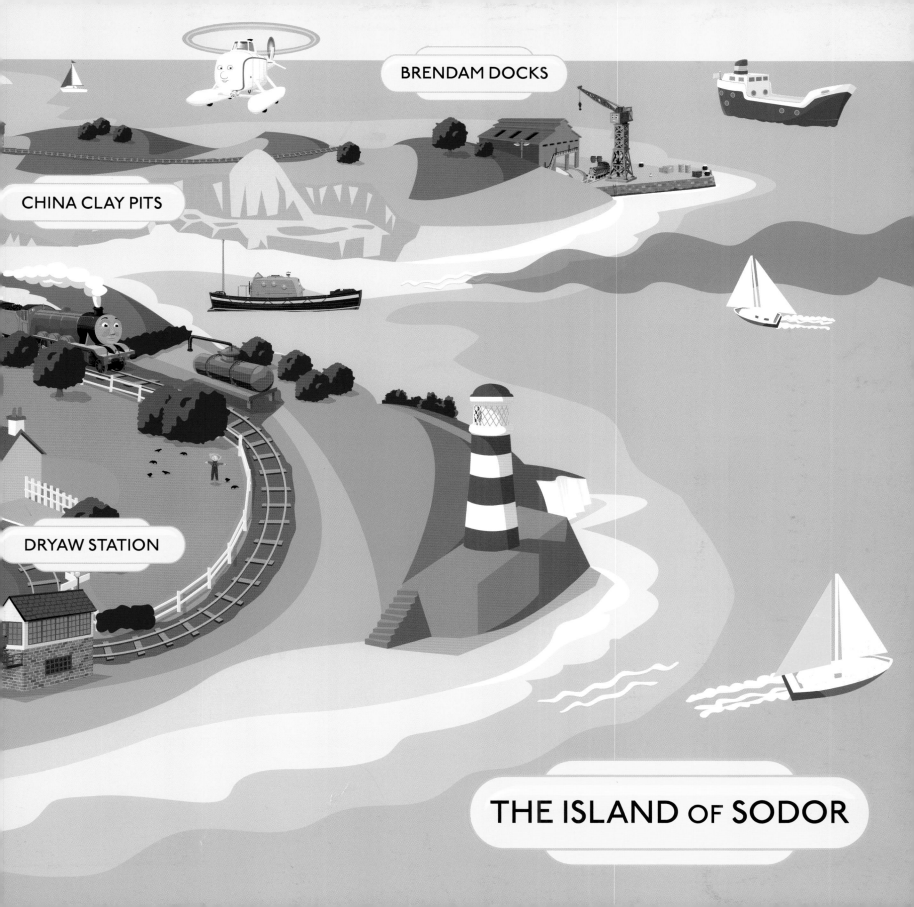

BRENDAM DOCKS

CHINA CLAY PITS

DRYAW STATION

THE ISLAND OF SODOR

About the creator

The Reverend W. Awdry was the creator of 26 little books about Thomas and his famous engine friends, the first being published in 1945. The stories came about when the Reverend's two-year-old son Christopher was ill in bed with the measles. Awdry invented stories to amuse him, which Christopher then asked to hear time and time again. And all these years later, children around the world continue to ask to hear these stories about Thomas, Edward, Gordon, James and the many other Really Useful Engines.

The Three Railway Engines,
first published in 1945.

The Reverend Awdry with some of his
readers at a model railway exhibition.